The Blood & The Glory

They overcame by the Blood of the Lamb and the word of their testimony

Revelation 12: 11

Phil Cawley

The Blood & The Glory

Well, You know, where I'm going

And God You know, oh where I've been

And there's no earthly way of knowing

What a price, to take away my sin

Through the blood and the glory

Sanctified and fit for the King

Through the blood and the glory

Thanks, and praises now we bring

The journey's long and the road is winding

The path that's straight is the Spirit's way

Through all the loosing and the binding

Our strength is in the Ancient of Days

The atonement of affection

Put the power into our faith

Through the blood, a hedge of protection

A wall of fire is going to keep us safe

Phil Cawley

Contents

Preface

Introduction

Chapter 1 Blood sacrifice

Chapter 2 Blood sacrifice defiled

Chapter 3 The Blood & the Glory

Chapter 4 The Cross, Blood & Resurrection

Chapter 5 Power in the Blood

Chapter 6 Healing in the Bood

Chapter 7 Freedom in the Blood

Chapter 8 Hedge of protection

Chapter 9 Feasting on the Blood

Chapter 10 Judged by the Blood

Chapter 11 Why Plead the blood

Chapter 12 Applying & Pleading the Blood

Conclusion

Preface

The Blood & The Glory is a no nonsense, no hole's barred, no skirting around the issue, no fear of what others may say, straight shooting book about the essence of Christianity. It may not meet the approval of some Christians, or Churches who want a motivational and uplifting message on a Sunday, before coffee and socialising with friends. It certainly will not meet the approval of those who sadly, and misguidedly, think that there are many ways to God, and that all paths eventually merge. It will not sit well with the many who are fence sitters, ambivalent, undecided or out and out atheist, as it will challenge, and shake up weak and flaky faith, and may well pierce through the conscience and hearts of the professing unbeliever.

This book is designed to be offensive; the blood of Jesus is the offense of the cross and does away with all legalism and pious religiosity. Only by faith are you saved through grace, and not by good works in case anyone should boast. The blood sacrifice of Jesus Christ atoned for all sin for those who repent and believe. The blood of Jesus took away all the power of sin, death, hell and the grave and put Satan on the run with time running out. The blood is the power of life within us and without it there is no life. How much more then, is the power of the blood of Jesus, the Son of God. His blood not only redeemed us from sin, but is the most powerful weapon for believers against all the powers of the kingdom of darkness. When we plead the blood, demons and devils flee.

The blood of Jesus speaks a better word (Hebrews 12: 24).

Introduction

Blood represents life in our bodies, it is constantly circulating and delivering the life-giving oxygen and nutrients we need to live and be healthy. Blood is a highly advanced communication and transport system which delivers messages to vital organs, bringing power, energy, health and nutrition. It is essential to the function of every cell in the body providing food and energy. The blood provides the perfect environment for the body to operate in optimal capacity. Blood is not only the life of the body, but also its protection, being an integral part of the immune system and highly complex. The life of the flesh and the whole body is in the blood and its function is astounding.

The divine life in the blood represents covenant, passion and the evidence of created existence. "For the life of the flesh is in the blood, and I have given it to you on the alter to make atonement for your souls, for it is the blood that makes atonement by the life" (Leviticus 17: 11). This is why the Children of Israel were forbidden, strictly commanded not to eat the blood of animals because it contained life.

Given the importance and central role of blood in the life and health of human beings, it should come as no great surprise, even to the uninitiated, of the central focus, power and importance of the blood of Jesus throughout the Bible. Without the saving, cleansing and healing power of the shed blood of Jesus, as the sacrifice for sins, there would be no Christianity. If the blood sacrifice and the redemptive power of the blood is not the focal point of believers; then they have missed the point, and will not be walking in power. We are told in the book of Timothy to avoid the kind of people who have a form of Godliness but deny the power (2 Timothy 3:5).

According to DL Moody, "the moment a man breaks away from this doctrine of the blood, religion becomes a sham, because the whole teaching in the Bible is of one story, and that is, that Christ came into this world and died for our sins." He went on to say that "the most solemn truth in the gospel, is that the only thing Christ left down here is His blood." Whenever the blood is preached about, talked about, or sung about, the power of the Holy Spirit will preside.

When the Roman Soldier plunged his spear into Jesus's side and blood came forth, sin was conquered, the blood covered the sin, the epitome of wickedness brought forth the essence of love. Many of the 'old timers' in Christian ministry, including Dr Alexander of Princeton College, would often say "make much of the blood"; without it you have a weak religion, that limps along.

Billye Brim wrote a book many years ago called The Blood and the Glory, and it so inspired me, that all these years later I have written an album, and now a book of the same title (hope she doesn't mind). In her book, Billye tells of another 'old timer' called Carl Roos, who, before he died, said "The Lord told us. Make much of the blood, and the blood will make much of you." The concept of honouring the blood of Jesus was very well known to these early Christians, and this was reflected in the songs they would sing. The presence of the Holy Spirit was always very strong in these meetings and signs and wonders would always manifest as a result. I have personally witnessed this all-consuming presence of God years back when the 'Toronto blessing' as it was called, was pouring out all over the world. I was attending a church in Sunderland at the time Pastored by Ken Gott, we sang many songs about the blood and the power and presence invoked was tangible.

The devil knows all too well about the power in the blood and the name of Jesus, and because he has no power to create, he tries to copy God's principles of power. There are many occult sects across the world who practice blood sacrifice, be that animal or human, and they abuse God's sacramental practices in their offerings to invoke the devil and evil spirits. The devil is fully aware of the power of the blood of Jesus, and he knows that a fervent church who practice this doctrine in their preaching and their praise and worship would be unstoppable. The devil and his scheming demons have worked their way into many church environments, and as a result rendered some of them powerless. For true revival to come, and it is coming, we need to get back to the power of the blood.

In this book I will be looking at the recorded historical context of blood sacrifice and the importance of this practice in worship and during feasts and ritual. I will also look at how these principles and practices have been abused and twisted for the devil's purposes and used in occult ritual. I will then be giving a detailed account of the ultimate sacrifice of Jesus which put an end to all future sacrificial worship. The rest of this short book will be primarily focusing on the power of the blood in communion, in healing, in deliverance, and in protection, and how to apply the blood of Jesus over every area of your life. There will be some prayers at the end of this book which you can use and adapt to apply the blood, or plead the blood over every facet of your life. All the Christians who are regularly appropriating the blood of Jesus over their lives, with full acceptance of all that it covers and provides, will live a life of victory and power in all their endeavours.

1   Blood Sacrifice

The need for sacrifice begins back in the early part of Genesis which tells of the fall of man. The disobedience of Adam and Eve introduced first sin ever committed by man and it followed the enticement of the devil in serpent guise. The serpent was crafty and planted seeds of doubt into Adam and Eve and they disobeyed God's command. Adam and Eve had been told by God that everything in the Garden of Eden was at their disposal, but they were not to eat from the tree of the knowledge of good and evil, for if they did, they would surely die. Satan tempted Eve to eat of the fruit of the tree saying, surely you will not die, but your eyes will be opened like God's knowing good and evil. Eve saw that the fruit was good and desiring wisdom she ate of it and gave some also to Adam. Adam and Eve were meant to live forever in perfect communion with God, living in paradise, but they ate of the forbidden tree because of the devils lies and manipulation. Satan had been cast out of Heaven because of his conceit and self-aggrandisement and his passionate desire to be equal with God. In the form of a serpent now he is bitterly jealous of man's closeness and relationship with God, so is hell-bent on sabotaging it. The serpent achieved his diabolical assignment and sin entered the world.

With the sin of man came the first sacrifice. Fig leaves were only a temporary fix for Adam and Eves newly discovered shame of their nakedness. Animal skin was now needed to permanently clothe Adam and Eve because their eyes had been opened. Adam and Eve could only be clothed by the shedding of blood. "The Lord God made garments of skin for Adam and his wife and clothed them" (Genesis 3: 21). Adam and Eve had been living side by side with all the animals in peace, and Adam had even been given the privilege of naming them all, but this was set to change. The act of killing then permeated the next generation with Adam's son Cain killing Abel because of jealousy. This trend continued and more sin entered the world on an ever-increasing rate and severity. The fallen angels, or Nephilim, were now breeding with the daughters of Men, and a population of half-breeds, or hybrids and giants were now growing in number. God at this point regretted creating mankind and saw no alternative but to wipe out the human race; so, He sent the great flood to the earth, sparing only Noah and his family.

God saw a void between Himself, a Holy God and his created race of sinful men, and He wanted a means of reconciliation. Sin and violence continued to be rampant amongst His people, but He ultimately called them out of captivity to follow Him, and to learn how to become a holy nation. Sinful man could not stand in the presence of such a holy God so some kind of covering would again be needed, just like with Adam and Eve. God gave many laws for His people to abide by but they kept on failing to keep them, so God introduced blood sacrifice, a sacrificial offering to atone for the sins of the people. This process would be something the people would repeat regularly to atone for their wrong doing.

The blood sacrifice was the ritualised slaughter of certain animals as pleasing offerings to God, it was symbolic of life and death. The only reason that animal sacrifice was acceptable to God was that it was a symbolic representation of the sacrifice of His Son which would ultimately be needed. The animals were prepared in certain ways and there were many specific rules around this process which had to be followed precisely. The sprinkling of blood represented life cleansing and the death of sin, as blood represented life. The reason for the blood sacrifice was that every book in the Old Testament pointed towards the great blood sacrifice of Jesus on behalf of mankind.

A sacrifice is the practice of offering up to God something precious, in exchange for their atonement, without the blood there was no forgiveness. So, life has to be lost so that atonement can be made. Often a goat would be separated from the other goats and used for sacrifice, a 'scapegoat', this goat would pay the price for the others. The animal sacrificed, whether goat, ox or lamb, had to be perfect, without defect or blemish in any way. The Old Testament blood sacrifices clearly symbolise what was to come later, in the crucifixion of Jesus as a sacrifice for all. The early blood sacrifices were a temporary thing, a practice that needed to be repeated, but the sacrifice Jesus made was the ultimate sacrifice to end the need for any more. "When Jesus had received the sour wine, He said it is finished, and He bowed His head and gave up His spirit" (John 19:30). When Jesus said it is finished, He was referring to the need for any further sacrifice, the ultimate price for sin had now been paid.

"The law required that nearly everything be cleansed with blood and that without the shedding of blood there is no remission for sin" (Hebrews 9:22). "He himself bore our sins in His own body on the cross, so that we might die to sins and be alive to righteousness; by His wounds you have been healed" (1 Peter 2: 24).

In the Old Testament the Lord gave strict commands against the consumption of blood. In Leviticus 17: 10 God says "I will set my face against any Israelite, or foreigner residing among them who eats blood, and I will cut them off from the people." He then goes on to explain his reasoning. "For the life of the flesh is in the blood, and I have given it to you on the alter to make atonement for your souls, for it is the blood that makes atonement by the life" (Leviticus 17: 11). Blood is the representation of life and without it no created being can live. God made blood sacrifice a part of His sacrificial system for the Jewish people, each sacrifice reminded them of the reality of life and death.

The blood sacrifice of the Jews became a symbol of freedom as it related to the Israelites freedom from Egypt. Each family on the first Passover would share a meal together consisting of lamb, and they would put some of the blood on the doorposts of the house to keep their family from losing their firstborn son, the blood symbolised life, death and freedom. Blood sacrifices came at a cost, the purchase of the animal was a reminder of this and represented the cost of sin. This blood covering for the sin of mankind offered a way for man to approach God, there had to be a death to atone for the Israelites sin and rebellion and so that they could gain forgiveness from God.

Many centuries went by and the rebellion of the Israelites continued, resulting in wars and famine, sexual deviance, idolatry, and oppression. God's chosen people survived as a scattered nation until the days and rule of the Roman Empire. The Israelites or children of God, were now more commonly referred to as the Jews. The Jews definitely still maintained some form of moral compass and were aware of their generational and present-day sins, and that forgiveness from their sins required a blood sacrifice. What sacrifice could ever be significant enough now to cover the sins of man.

Then Jesus came, and was here on assignment from God. Jesus came to the earth to give His life for the salvation of many. Jesus was perfect, without sin or defect of any kind, He was the perfect sacrifice and the saviour of mankind. This would be the sacrifice to end all sacrifices, to put an end to the power of sin, hell, and death.

The grave could not hold Him, He stripped away the power of darkness and rose victorious, Commander of the Angel armies of God.

2 Blood sacrifice defiled

The devil is a defeated foe, his time is running out. Unfortunately, he is the god of this world. "Satan, who is the god of this world, has blinded the minds of those who don't believe" (2 Corinthians 4: 4). Satan is a weaver of lies, he likes to convince people that he doesn't exist, this is his greatest trick, and with most people he has got it in the bag. Satan or the devil is real, he is a thief and his mission is to steal, kill and destroy (John 10: 10). It appears, on face value, that he is doing a great job at the moment in fulfilling his mission.

We are seeing an unprecedented death toll with the current world pandemic. Astronomical financial loss to world finances as a result of excessive pressure on health services, mass job losses and business closure. New levels of corruption are being seen within government bodies; Christian leaders having their power stolen in favour of communist sympathisers and fraternisers. Christian values and morals are being undervalued or totally removed from our schools and colleges; foundational Christian integrity is becoming almost invisible in government, or at best is being seen as extremism. The devil's assignment to kill, steal and destroy seems like a fait accompli, and the loss of life incurred recently would represent unprecedented sacrifice for the devil's schemes. Remember, he comes to steal, kill and destroy!

Following on from the story of the birth of Jesus in the New Testament of the Bible we saw the anti-Christ agenda of king Herod. Herod had been notified of the birth of Jesus and he initiated the murder of all infants in Bethlehem in an attempt to kill the baby Jesus. We read in the book of Mathew how Herod was tricked by the wise men as they were supposed to inform him when they found Jesus. Herod was furious and he had his men kill all the male children in Bethlehem and the surrounding region, two years old and younger. The devil always demands his sacrifices, he is a copy-cat and counterfeit who wanted to emulate God so much that he wanted to equal Him. What a blood sacrifice, the mass slaughter of thousands of babies and toddlers in pursuit of the impossible task of removing Jesus.

There are many examples in the Bible of the devil demanding blood sacrifice, and the many followers of these satanic cults have been required to provide blood sacrifices to appease him. God in the Old Testament used the blood sacrifice of animals, so Satan copies this ritual but uses a twisted version, human sacrifice. The people involved in the cults that practiced this have readily made these great and hideous sacrifices. Child sacrifice was deemed to be an indication of how devout a person was to serving their satanic pagan gods and they were willing to offer the most important things in life to please these evil deities. The devil comes to steal, kill and destroy, it's his mission, and he was ticking all three boxes by deluding his followers to adopt such diabolical rituals.

Sacrifices to the Canaanite god Molech were strongly condemned in the Bible. "Thou shalt not give any of thy seed to set them apart to Molech" (Leviticus 18: 21). These ancient rites were described with horror in another passage of scripture. "They built high places to Baal in the valley of Beth-Hinnom and immolated their son's and daughter's to Molech bringing sin upon Judah, this I never commanded them, nor did it enter my mind that they should practice such abominations" (Jerimiah 32:35). The death penalty was often the price paid for sacrificial worship of this nature in the Old Testament. In Leviticus we read that any Israelite who gives his offspring to Molech shall be put to death by stoning as he has profaned the holy name of God.

History has shown many reports of blood sacrifice to appease their Satanic deities. The Aztecs sacrificed tens of thousands of prisoners in ceremonies to consecrate the great pyramids. Some cultures follow a 'retainer sacrifice' having wives, servants and concubines killed at their funeral, under the notion that they can take them all with them into their afterlife. Mongols, Scythians and early Egyptians believed they could take all their household with them to serve them in the afterlife. Headhunting was practiced by many tribal cultures where heads were taken for ceremonial and magical purposes.

Satan has continued in his quest to pervert the will of God since he was first banished from Heaven with his fallen angels. There has been a continuation of bloodshed and sacrifice of life ever since. He has his ways and schemes, subtle and crafty, and he weaves them into the minds of men to carry out his diabolical plans in a desperate bid to try to somehow discredit God and disprove the Bible.

Many pointless wars have been fought bringing mass sacrifice of life and many evil men have been used to orchestrate such devastating and horrific bloodshed. Hitler would be a prime example or this being a known follower of occult beliefs and practicing magic, along with many others within the higher ranks of the Nazi regime. History shows that Hitler made extensive notes on a book called Magic: Theory, History and Practice, and he had underlined passages like, "He who does not carry demonic seeds within him will never give birth to a new world". This was a book by Ernst Schertel a German who was into mysticism, and was a researcher into alternative sexual practices and the occult. He sent Hitler a copy of this book in 1923 when it was finished. Hitler was the epitome of evil and made a great sacrifice to his father the devil, by sacrificing six million Jews in his concentration camps. Hitler had the notion that if he could wipe out the Jewish race, then he could do the devil's work and prove that the Bible and God's plans were wrong. If all Jews were wiped out, then how could God's chosen people return to their homeland of Israel and come back to God. Hitler tried his best to make this evil scheme come into fruition but it was never going to happen, not while there is a God in Heaven! The Jews are now returning to their homeland in great numbers and have been since Hitlers defeat.

There have been endless blood sacrifices made throughout history and still continue to this day. Evil men and women possessed by demonic spirits and devils to carry out these abominations. Spree killings, mass murders, serial murders, drive by shootings. War crimes, virus and biological warfare, chemical weapons, suicide bombers and terrorist attacks from extremist religious groups.

There are many occult sects who still use animal and human sacrifice in their devil worship because they recognise the power in the blood and they are appropriating this for evil purpose. This is not only a widespread practice in third world countries and in voodoo cultures, with practicing witch doctors, it is prevalent across many areas of the world and crosses all socio-economic groups. I will go further into this in future writing. Needless to say, the devil is alive and well and making the most of his ever-depleting time allowance before his free reign comes to an end.

3 The Blood & the Glory

"But I have come that they may have life and have it more abundantly" (John 10: 10). "The reason the Son of God appeared was to destroy all the works of the devil" (1 John 3: 8).

God revealed His plan for the salvation of mankind from the beginning. He knew that when He created man that He would have to give man freewill, so that man could choose to follow his creator. God also knew that mankind would fall, would get it wrong, would stray from the path of righteousness and do evil deeds that would cause a void between him and God. God had already planned for this; he had a contingency plan ready for when this would happen. "For God so loved the world, that He gave His only begotten Son, that whosoever believes in Him, will not perish, but will have everlasting life" (John 3: 16). This was always the plan; Jesus was referred to in the book of Revelation as "The Lamb that was slain from the foundation of the world." So, God's perfect plan was in place, He knew that with freewill, man would fail, but He loved man regardless and unconditionally. This was not a plan pulled together because of man's failure, it was all foreknown and pre-planned.

Jesus's birth was foretold throughout the old testament "The virgin will conceive and give birth to a son, and will call Him Immanuel" (Isaiah 7: 14). The bloodline of Jesus was clearly marked out through the Old Testament and often, against all odds, the bloodline continued where it seemed impossible and the men and women of God kept their faith until Jesus was born.

Jesus's death too was prophesised hundreds of years before it came to pass. Jesus came into the world to save sinners and to undo all the works of the devil. In Zechariah 13: 7 it is written "God will strike the Shepherd and the sheep will be scattered", obviously referring here to Jesus, the Good Shepherd. In Isaiah 53: 7 we read "He was led like a lamb to the slaughter, and as a sheep is silent before its shearers, He never said a word." King David wrote in the book of Psalms 900 B.C. before crucifixion had been invented "My enemies surround me like a pack of dogs, an evil gang closes in on me, they have pierced my hands and feet" (Psalm 22: 16). Isaiah 50: 6 says "I offered my back to those who beat me and my cheeks to those who pulled out my beard, I did not hide my face from mockery and spitting". Psalm 69: 21 states "They offer me sour wine for my thirst." There are numerous references to the purposed death of Jesus throughout scripture as this was His ultimate assignment, to pay for the sins of men and to defeat all the power and works of the devil. Jesus spoke many times to His disciples about the fact that He would have to suffer many things at the hands of the elders and chief priests and that he would suffer and die, but that on the third day He would rise again. Jesus tried to make the disciples understand that His life would be given as a ransom or sacrifice for many.

Jesus could have had power over any of the situations he found Himself in, but He was only interested in doing the will of the Father.

Jesus prayed earnestly to God on the Mount of Olives before His arrest and His sweat was like drops of blood falling to the floor. When the soldiers led by Judas came to arrest Him, they asked for Jesus, He answered "I am He" and they all fell backwards to the ground as they felt His authority. This is The Son of God. When Judas saw that Jesus had been condemned, he threw the money back to the chief priests and elders and went away and hanged himself, this was also prophesied in the book of Jeremiah.

Jesus was put on trial for claiming to be the king of the Jews, this was seen as rebellion by the Jews, and punishable only by death. When Jesus was asked if He was the king of the Jews, He answered "You have said so". Though Pontious Pilate had reservations, and could find no wrong in Jesus, he had to please the people by giving in to their request. Even Pilate's wife warned him saying, don't have anything to do with this innocent man for I have suffered a great deal in a dream because of Him. Pilate washed his hands in front of the people to symbolise that he was not taking responsibility for the blood of this man, then handed Jesus over to be beaten and lashed. They called together the whole company of soldiers. A crown made of thorns was forced upon His head and they put a purple robe on Him, they mocked Him saying "Hail king of the Jews". They spat on Him and struck Him repeatedly with their fists and staffs. He was flogged, beaten and lashed until unrecognisable. They put His own clothes back on Him and He was made to carry a heavy cross to the place of crucifixion. When they had nailed Him to the cross between two thieves, they put a sign above Him with a charge saying 'This is Jesus, The King of the Jews'. The high priests wanted the sign to be changed to say He claims to be king of the Jews, but Pilate said, what I have written, I have written. Many watching mocked Him saying, you saved others, save yourself, come down from the cross and we will believe you.

Jesus could have stepped down from the cross at any time He chose, He could have called down legions of Angels to His assistance and destroyed the government and all the persecutors. Instead, Jesus said "Father forgive them for they know not what they do." Soldiers played dice games for his clothes and he hung on a cross between two thieves as prophesied. One of the criminals hanging next to Jesus said to Him "if you are the Messiah save yourself and us", the other criminal rebuked him and said, "Don't you fear God, we deserve our punishment, this man has done nothing wrong." Then he said to Jesus, "remember me when you come into Your kingdom", Jesus answered him saying "Truly I tell you, this day you will be with me in paradise."

At 3 in the afternoon Jesus cried out in a loud voice "Eli Eli, lema sabachthani" which means "My God, my God, why have You forsaken me." Some watching thought He was calling on Elijah, one of them put wine vinegar on a sponge and lifted it on a staff for Jesus to drink. Others said leave Him alone, let's see if Elijah comes to His aid. Jesus said "It is finished", with that He bowed His head and gave up His spirit. There was a centurion standing nearby Jesus, and when he saw how Jesus died he said "surely, this man was the Son of God".

When Jesus died darkness covered the whole land. In the book of Amos 8: 9 we read "In that day, says the Sovereign Lord, I will make the sun go down at noon and darken the earth while it is still day." The darkness lasted from 12 noon until 3 pm while Jesus was on the cross. At the moment of His final breath, the earth shook, the temple curtain was ripped in two from top to bottom, and the tombs of many of the saints of God were opened up and the bodies raised to life. It wasn't just Pilate now who would have had reservations, what a dramatic scene and atmosphere. Something monumental had just taken place, the world would never be the same again. What about the families or relatives of the saints who had been raised from the dead, the place must have been buzzing with conversation in awe and wonder of the events of that great and fearful day.

4 The Cross, Blood & Resurrection

A blood sacrifice had to be made for the atonement of the sins of mankind. Animal sacrifice was no longer enough. The blood shed to take away the sins of the world had to come from a spotless lamb, the perfect sacrifice, the Lamb slain from the foundation of the world. Jesus Christ – God in human form, all man, all flesh but still God, was the only sacrifice fitting for the redemption of sin. This was the perfect plan of God, to send His Son to die on a cross, shed His blood to pay the price, then rose again having conquered sin, death and the grave to sit at the right hand of God. "Surely He hath borne our griefs, and carried our sorrows: But He was wounded for our transgressions, bruised for our iniquities: the chastisement of our peace was upon Him; and by His stripes we are healed" (Isaiah 53: 4-5). Jesus in His sacrificial death took our grief and sorrows and purchased our healing and deliverance.

The cross on which Jesus died is symbolic, it is an alter to God. The cross is sometimes referred to as a tree and scripture tells us that "cursed is anyone who hangs from a tree" (Galatians 3: 13). Jesus became cursed for us and bore all our iniquities that we would be free from the curse of sin and death. "The wages of sin is death, but the gift of God is eternal life" (Romans 6: 23). The gift of God is Jesus and what He did for us on the cross to secure the eternal future for all who believe." The cross is symbolic of the door posts on the homes of the Israelites during Passover. The Israelites had to sacrifice a lamb for their family to eat and apply some of the blood on the doorposts of their homes. When God sent the Angel of death to fly over, he would kill all the firstborn sons of the Egyptians, but would spare the Israelites as he would see the blood on their doorposts and Passover. Jesus is the spotless lamb and His blood was freely given on the cross to account for our sins. When we believe in Jesus and his death and resurrection we are covered by His blood. God no longer sees our sins and our iniquities; all He sees is the blood of Jesus and so we are accepted as sons and daughters of God into His family.

Without the resurrection of Jesus this would have been a sacrifice in vain, the power of sin, death and the grave would have remained as powerful as ever. The wages of our sin would still have been death, but thankfully God's master plan was perfect, Jesus was raised from the dead on the third day by the power of the Holy Spirit. The best part about this is that the same power that raised Jesus from the dead lives in us. Jesus's blood is applied to the mercy seat of Heaven as the perfect sacrifice, Jesus has done this as our High Priest. The blood of Jesus speaks a better word, and God always hears it.

There has been some discussion about where Jesus was during the time between His death and His resurrection as there is very little in scripture about this period. Most scholars gravitate towards the passage in 1 Peter 3: 18 which talks about Jesus proclaiming to the spirits imprisoned. There doesn't seem to be any hard and fast conclusion on this despite much debate. I tend to subscribe to the teaching I heard from Kat Kerr which was given to her in revelation from God. Kats revelation is based around the scripture in Colossians 2. Reading from verse 12 we see the discourse about believers being buried with Christ in baptism and raised with Him through faith in God who raised Him from the dead. It continues to say we were made alive in Christ from the forgiveness of sins, having had our legal debts cancelled by nailing our debt to the cross. Jesus then, having disarmed the powers and authorities, or having spoiled the principalities and powers, He made a show of them openly, triumphing over them in it. In this way He disarmed spiritual rulers and shamed them publicly by His victory on the cross. So, the inference is, (and Kat would agree), that following His death on the cross, Jesus went into Hell took away the keys of sin, death and the grave from the devil, and made a spectacle of him openly. Kat would add that he ridiculed the devil and melted the faces of the demons. I'm sticking with Kat's version of events; it sounds like what Jesus would do.

All our sins and corruption were nailed to the cross as Jesus took them upon Himself and willingly went to the altar. Jesus took away the sting of death by defeating Satan, and all the powers of darkness, and stripping him of the keys by providing eternal life through His blood. Jesus was raised up into His body again on the third day by the power of the Holy Spirit.

Easter Sunday is the most important day in the Christian calendar. The resurrection of Jesus brings power and hope of a future and of eternal life. In Mathew's gospel, he describes a mighty earthquake as an angel of the Lord descended to earth and to the tomb of Jesus, and rolled away the stone. The angel was bright as lightening and the guards of the tomb were terrified, they shook and became like dead men. The angel spoke to the women telling them not to be afraid but to inform the disciples that their Lord has risen as He said He would. There is some variation across the 4 gospels regarding this account but the essence is the same. The angel or angels are saying don't look for the living among the dead, Jesus has risen. Jesus is sited to appear to the women in Mathew and John's gospel and told to tell the disciples. The individual detail here is less important than the over-riding fact that Jesus is alive.

Jesus was on the earth for 40 days between His resurrection and His ascension and He appeared to his disciples 10 times, 5 of which were on the day of His resurrection. According to the first chapter of the book of Acts, Jesus presented Himself to His disciples with much convincing proof that He was indeed alive, He spoke mainly about the Kingdom of God. Mary Magdalene saw Him first and He called her by name. He then appeared to a group of women who had been with Mary in the graveyard, they came to Him and worshipped at His feet. Later, on the road to Emmaus, Jesus appeared to two disciples and they didn't recognise Him until he broke bread with them. They commented afterwards how their hearts had been burning with passion as He had been speaking to them on the journey. Jesus then appeared to them in a locked room, they were hiding for fear of the authorities, He said "Peace be with you", they thought He was a ghost. Jesus showed them His hands and His pierced side, He said "see, a ghost does not have flesh and bones" and they were overjoyed, Jesus breathed on them and said, receive the Holy Spirit. Jesus revealed Himself again when Thomas was present, as he had heard the good news but not believed and wanted to touch physical evidence, Jesus instructed Thomas to stop doubting (John 20: 27). Jesus appeared to the disciples again while they were fishing and performed another miracle giving them an enormous catch, He speaks privately with Peter and restores his faith.

Jesus gave His disciples the great commission to go into the world and make disciples of all nations, baptising in the name of the Father, the Son and the Holy Spirit. These signs will follow those who believe; in My name they will drive out demons, speak in new tongues, pick up deadly snakes and no poison will harm them. They will place their hands on the sick people and they will be healed.

After Jesus had said all these things to His disciples in the vicinity of Bethany, He lifted up His hands and blessed them. While He was still blessing them, He was taken from them and ascended into Heaven. "And it came to pass, while He blessed them, He parted from them, and was carried up to Heaven Then they worshiped Him and returned to Jerusalem with great joy" (Luke 24:51-52). So, 40 days after His resurrection, Jesus left the earth, being taken up, body and soul, to Heaven to re-join God the

Father and it was witnessed by the eleven remaining disciples. The disciples were renewed in their spirits and went away worshiping God in continuous praise.

Look to the cross:

When you taste the bitter waters in your life, look to the cross. When the world is falling over in your sight, look to the cross. You'll find your freedom, you'll find your peace, look to the cross.

When you need a touch of healing in your life, look to the cross. When your beating heart is bleeding deep inside, look to the cross. Nailed to the tree, He set you free, He took the stripes, He paid the fee, look to the cross.

New life You breathe, You told me, and all authority is yours. New life you breathe You showed me, where there's no way, You open doors. You transcend time, You right the wrongs, You heal us body, mind and soul. When we are weak, then You are strong, You take the broken and make it whole. Nothing is impossible for You.

(Phil Cawley)

5 Power in the blood

The reason the that the blood of Jesus is so powerful is because it is breathed straight from the mouth of God. God breathed life into Adam and his blood stream was pure, but he committed sin and his blood was corrupted. Jesus could not have any of Mary's blood within Him as her blood was also corrupted due to the fall of man. Jesus was conceived through the Holy Spirit, His blood is the pure and divine breath of God. The blood has power because the blood of Jesus and the Holy Spirit are connected, the blood and the breath of God are interconnected. Where the blood is, the Holy Spirit will manifest and where the blood is the word is. There is agreement between the word, the Spirit and the blood. Your blood keeps you alive because it has the life of God in it, without this you die, when your spirit, (which is you) leaves the body, the body dies and the blood decays.

Your blood keeps your body alive; His blood keeps your spirit alive. God made a covenant to save mankind, and the ultimate blood covenant and blood sacrifice was Jesus, God in flesh. The covenant between the divine and the human, sealed by the blood of animals, had always been broken by the weakness and sin of men. God needed to make a different covenant, so He became flesh, as a man, so that on behalf of man He could make a covenant with Himself, sealed by the Holy Spirit, and it can never be broken. "I have sworn by myself; the word has gone out of my mouth in righteousness, and shall not return. That unto me every knee shall bow, every tongue shall swear" (Isaiah 45: 23).

Jesus shed His blood seven times for us. First in the garden of Gethsemane when His sweat became blood, this according to Benny Hinn was for the healing of our emotions. It was shed again in the house of Caiaphas where His beard was ripped from His face. Then He had the crown of thorns forced upon his head and shed blood for the healing of our minds, and protection from evil influences. He then had his back lacerated and His blood flowed, for the healing of all infirmities. Then on the cross they nailed His hands and his blood was shed for the work of our hands, and for our walk of righteousness when they nailed His feet. They pierced His side and blood flowed for the salvation of the church. The Christian church was born on that day as Jesus took away the sins of mankind.

We apply the blood by speaking it out, in the Old Testament they used branches of hyssop, we use our word. According to the book of Job, we can apply the blood to ourselves, our homes and families, our possessions, our work and our influence. We can get the favour of God over every work of our hands when we apply the blood of Jesus. We should make it a habit to practice this application every day, and receive blessing and favour, healing and protection as we go about our daily business and carry out our assignments. As a Christian you have full access to the pleading of the blood when you pray, and when you do apply the blood, the powers of darkness cannot come near you. Demons and devils cannot read your thoughts, they can only hear your words, but when you use your words and plead the blood in Jesus name, demons will flee. The book of Proverbs tells us in chapter 18:21 that the power of life and death are in the tongue, and they that love it shall eat the fruit thereof. We can speak either life or death over our lives. When we appropriate the power of the blood, we do so with the spoken word and devils will tremble. You must use your words, there is so much power in the spoken word, "let the redeemed of the Lord say so" (Psalm 107: 2). God said in the book of Isaiah 43: 1; "I have redeemed you, and called you by name, you are mine." So, if you are redeemed and called, and the possession of God, then you have power and protection in the blood.

All blood has a voice and when it cries out to God, He hears the cry. Abel's blood cried out for justice and got God's attention. Jesus' blood speaks a better word and it will overcome anything in your life; if God hears Abel's blood, how much more will hear Jesus. When the devil is presented with the voice of the blood of Jesus, he knows he is in real trouble. "When Christs blood takes the microphone, every square inch of the vast universe, every subterranean haunt of darkness, every hot and blackened corner of Hell, and every angel in the celestial choir, shut up and listen. When Christ's blood takes the microphone, it's the only sound in creation, the booming declaration that echoes down the corridors of time, saying, Father forgive them" Chad Bird.

Jesus said to God, "of those You have given me, I have lost none." (John 18: 9) When you apply, or plead the blood of Jesus, you are applying the life of Jesus, the Son of God over your problems and nothing in the world can come against, or escape the mighty power in the life of God. When you plead the blood of Jesus you instantly remind the enemy of his defeat at the cross of Jesus and how Jesus made a show of the devil openly and stripped away his power. This is the most powerful force in our spiritual warfare and in our prayers for healing and deliverance. When you use the blood of Jesus in this way, these are no ordinary words you are speaking, you are making an assault on Hell, with the power of The Almighty-God. When you pray in this way you need to understand the power you are invoking, and be fully expectant that your prayers, if they are in line with God's word, will be answered. When you plead the blood of Jesus, you will be healed, you will be delivered, this is a most powerful weapon. Pleading the blood in the name of Jesus is a mighty combination, as this is the name above all names, and every knee must bow.

God is infinite, all powerful, everlasting, timeless, the Architect of the universe, indestructible. When He puts His life into another being, that too becomes indestructible and everlasting. All created beings, therefore are eternal, even if they are bad, because they were created for good. The devil and his hoards are still living, God didn't kill them; He could have, instead He banished them, as He could allow no sin of any kind to tarnish Heaven. Everything breathed into life by God retains that life force. As children of the most-high God, we have the blood of Jesus running through our veins, we are adopted into His family as the redeemed of the Lord. We will all go through a physical death one day, but the body is just our earth suit, we are spirit, we have a soul (mind, will & emotions) and we live in a body. Our spirit man will live forever and we will be given a new heavenly body which will be perfect. We cannot die because of the life of God within us as created beings. The blood is the source of life, so, the blood of Jesus is the all-powerful source of life, indestructible, wielding all authority over any and every situation in our lives. Pleading the blood of Jesus then is not for the faint hearted, this is big league and carries the mighty arsenal of the hosts of Heaven.

Redemption through the blood of Jesus sanctifies, heals, restores and perfects us and gives us the promise of eternal life. Jesus Himself came by water and blood and the Spirit of truth testifies to this. The Spirit, the water and the blood are in agreement. "Those who have been chosen are pre-destined by the knowledge of God the Father, through the sanctifying work of the Spirit, to be obedient to Jesus Christ and sprinkled with His blood" (1 Peter 1: 2). Where the blood is, the Spirit is, the precious blood of Jesus is a conduit for the Holy Spirit. This is why the Holy Spirit moved so strongly in the church in years gone by. The Azusa Street saints, Catherine Kuhlman, Charles Finney and all the great revival tent and healing ministries knew the power of the blood and the anointing of the Holy Spirit.

"When we praise the name of Jesus, when we sing about the blood. We are sealed by His Spirit, and our prayers are understood. May our praises and worship, bring a glory cloud above. Let it rain Holy Spirit, refresh us with Your love." (Phil Cawley)

The power of the blood is the most powerful weapon in the spiritual warfare of Christians, but one of the least understood and utilised. In the book of 1 Peter 1:18-19 we read "we were not redeemed by corruptible things such as silver and gold, or by the vain traditions from our fathers, but with the precious blood of

Christ, as a lamb without spot or blemish." In the book of Revelation, we read "they overcame by the blood of the lamb and the word of their testimony, and they loved not their lives, even to death" (Revelation 12:10).

We are instructed by many of the 'old timers' and the Generals in the ministry to make much of the blood, or to plead the blood. The Hebrew translation of the word plead is 'Shaphat', which mean to strive or contend for, or make a legal case for. We are legally making our case to God through the blood of Jesus. We have legal right when we are redeemed through the blood. We have all committed many sins and iniquities throughout or lives, and we will continue to do so; but when we repent of our sins we are washed through the blood. God doesn't see our sins, He just sees the blood, and we are accepted into His family. When we plead the blood over our lives and our families, the devil has no legal rights to interfere and must leave us alone. The devils and demons fear and tremble when we plead the blood, using the name of Jesus, there is nothing more powerful. We have the greatest advocate, and the devil's case will be thrown out every time.

"There is nothing more factual, nothing more supernatural, than the blood of Jesus; nothing so powerful, no healing flow so wonderful as the blood of Jesus." (Phil Cawley)

Being redeemed by the blood of Jesus means that we are free from the curse of the law, free from poverty, lack and limitation. We are forgiven and cleansed by the blood, and we have remission from our sin; "This is my blood of the covenant, which is poured out for many for the forgiveness of sins" (Mathew 26:28). We are free from all guilt and shame. God sees the blood, "when I see the blood, I will pass over you, and the plague will not come upon you" (Exodus 12:13). God honours the blood, and when we plead with the blood, the Spirit will always manifest and God will always hear. To overcome means to conquer, to claim victory. So then, to make much of the blood, or plead the blood is presenting a case against the devil by pleading what the blood has done for us, and this will overcome the lies of the enemy. The blood is the river that carries the Holy Spirit according to Benny Hinn, when God breathed, a river of blood flowed through the veins of that first man. When the Holy Spirit breathed on the second Adam, it was the blood of God that flowed through Him, Jesus has the blood of God in His veins, it was this blood that was shed on the cross through Jesus. It was this blood that atoned for our sins and bought us into the family, as heirs of God.

"There's just something about the blood, Jesus Christ Son of God. There's Just something about that name, oh, His loss for my gain. There is power to set you free, plead the blood, demons flee." (Phil Cawley)

But we must know who we are in God, an heir is no different to a slave unless he has knowledge and understanding (Galations 4: 1). We need to know who we are in Christ, in order to be released from bondage. Then we will be able to walk in power and victory and fullness of life (Romans 6: 16). We have been told that we have all authority and that no harm can befall us, but we need to know who we are for this to be the case.

We are reconciled to God because of Jesus, we belong to Him, the power of the blood brings us into fellowship with the Father, God became mad in order to redeem us and put us in right standing with Him. We are cleansed by the blood, and when cleansing occurs, sin loses its power. We are also sanctified through the body of Jesus once and for all (Hebrews 10: 10).

6 Healing in the blood

"He was wounded for our transgressions, bruised for our iniquities: the chastisement of our peace was upon Him; and by His stripes we are healed." (Isaiah 53: 5).

When Jesus was scourged and whipped and lashed and His flesh was torn from His body, leaving great stripes, welts and gouges, His blood flowed down from these stripes. The precious, powerful, healing blood flowing from these wounds was now the sacrificial covering for mankind. This was the cost for the forgiveness of our sins and iniquities. The prolonged and torturous physical abuse inflicted on Jesus rendered Him to be unrecognisable, throughout this process of torture He was mocked and ridiculed, and then finally crucified. "He Himself bore our sins in His body on the cross, so that we might die to sins and live for righteousness; by His wounds you have been healed" (1 Peter 2: 24).

God sees our sin as a disease and He sent Jesus as the remedy for this. The word stripes is used to set forth His sufferings, both of body and soul. His mind and body suffered grief we can never fully understand or even describe, said Spurgeon. He was in emotional and spiritual agony and turmoil well before His actual death. Large drops of blood and sweat fell to the ground, few men have ever reached the depths of sweating blood, and who have would have been very close to their death; but Jesus lived through this to move on to a slow and agonising assault on His endurance. He was mocked and ridiculed and scourged. Scourging is one of the worst tortures that can be inflicted on a man, it digs out welts, as it tears and rips out the flesh. The Roman scourge was said to have been made of sinews taken from oxen and twisted into knots with insertions of bone protruding along its length. The Roman scourge split into 3 tails at the end to maximise its damage, so every lash was really three lashes, each with jagged bone pieces slashing and tearing as they landed on His skin. Every time He was whipped, furrows were created down the length of His back, and this was just the beginning for Jesus. In addition, they struck Him repeatedly in the face whilst mocking

Him and asking Him to prophesy which one had hit him. They then ripped out the beard from His face, imagine that experience alone guys. Totally exhausted, He was then forced to carry the weighty cross, which to anyone would be a burdensome task in its own right. Jesus was stripped and thrown down onto the splintered wood of the cross where His lacerated back would stain the wood with His blood. This again is very symbolic and depicts the lamb and the blood on the wooden alters of Old Testament times. Jesus was nailed hands and feet to the cross and the large structure was then jerked violently into its place in a prepared hole in the ground so that all His limbs were dislocated. This was to fulfil what was written in Psalm 22: 16, "Dogs surround me, a pack of villains encircles me, they pierce my hands and feet". "I am poured out like water, and all my bones are out of joint, my heart has turned to wax, melting within me" (Psalm 22: 14).

The weight of Jesus body says Spurgeon, would have at first been supported by His feet, until the nails tore through the tender nerves. Once this began, the painful load would begin to weigh on his pierced hands tearing at His flesh, dragging rusty metal nails tearing through fine bones and delicate flesh, while those around continued to mock and jeer at Him. Jesus had lost a lot of body fluid and was dehydrated. His tongue was sticking to the roof of His mouth (Psalm 22: 15). He asked for a drink and was given vinegar mixed with gall. At this point Jesus said "it is finished", and gave up His spirit.

As if crucifixion is not barbaric enough, on top of this, Jesus was carrying the weight of the sin and guilt of mankind, this was so heavy on His heart, but He was willing to pay the price for our redemption. Jesus, in his hours of agony could not even turn to God, He was alone completely, separated from God for the first time ever. He cried out, "My God, My God, why have You forsaken me" (Mathew 27: 46), a scripture echoing Psalm 42 :9. God, had to turn His back on sin, and Jesus was carrying the weight of it on His body on behalf of mankind.

Jesus willingly became the remedy for the disease of sin, but just like any other remedy, we must apply it to our lives, and we do this by believing, in faith, that He has paid the price for us. We will not ever have to pay the price for our sin, it has been paid, and this one payment is all sufficient.

It is widely believed that Jesus received the same punishment as a common criminal, which was the full 40 lashes minus one, as it was believed that 40 or more would kill a man. Some believe that the number of lashes given to Jesus, represent the number of root causes of disease known to man, and that blood was shed for each one. There is no real evidence that this is the case. Jesus, by His stripes and His cruel death bought spiritual and physical healing for all who believe. Rapha is the original word used for the healing nature of God. Jehovah Rapha is God's power to heal you physically, emotionally, mentally and spiritually and is the root word of many of the healing verses in the Bible. This word is multi-faceted, but broadly speaking, it is referring to wholesomeness of health.

Cleansing is a vital part to the healing process of God. "If we confess our sins. He is faithful and just to forgive us our sins and cleanse us from all unrighteousness" (1 John 1: 9). "The blood of Jesus Christ His Son, cleanses us from all sin." (1 John 1: 7). In the same way, the blood of Jesus can cleanse us from all disease and sickness and all other things coming from the fallen nature of man, but thankfully we have the full assurance, that, by His stripes we are healed. Jesus blood shed for us bringing miraculous healing power, it is potent when applied to your given situation in faith. Jesus earthly 'parents' were Mary and Joseph, but His real parentage came from the Holy Spirit who over shadowed Mary, bringing an immaculate conception. Jesus was a man of flesh, just as we are, but the blood running through His veins was supernatural. He was in no way corrupted by any historical bloodline. The blood of Jesus then is divinely pure and potent and can set any prisoner free. His blood can cure any cancer, or heart disease, any illness, addiction or virus, either known or not yet invented. His blood avails for many, His blood avails for me.

Many Christians today seem to have great difficulty in accepting that God is still in the healing business. There is often the notion amongst believers that healing miracles of the Bible not only originated in Biblical times, but also finished or ceased at the end of the New Testament. Christians who adopt this misguided view are often referred to as 'cessationists'. Some cessationists would also include some of the spiritual gifts like prophecy, and speaking in tongues, and assert that all these things ceased with the Apostolic Age. Nowhere in the Bible will you find evidence that healing, deliverance, or any of the other spiritual gifts were for Biblical times only. Christians are wrong to be 'cherry picking' which parts of the Bible to believe, and which parts to have 'their own view on'. Ephesians 4: 11- 13 tells us to pursue spiritual gifts for the building up of the body of Christ until we all come into the unity of faith and of the knowledge of the Son of God, into a complete man to the measure and the fullness of Christ. I'm not sure about you, but I am definitely not measuring up to the fullness of Christ yet! There are many verses in scripture which are clear teaching to Christians. Mathew 10: 6-8 could not be any clearer, Jesus is speaking to His disciples and says "go to the lost sheep of Israel and proclaim this message: The Kingdom of Heaven has drawn near. Heal the sick, raise the dead, cleanse those with leprosy, drive out demons. Freely you have received, freely give" I have looked in all translations of the Bible and cannot find anywhere the caveat that states 'only for use in New Testament times'. So, for me, I will follow what Jesus said until He tells me otherwise. Sorry for the slight digression, but that needed to be said as things like that can be very damaging to new Christians.

Another problem some Christians face is regarding the receiving of their healing. Sometimes when the power of the Holy Spirit is thick in a meeting, healing manifestation may be instant and obvious so there is no problem in believing. In the meetings at Azusa Street for example, everything was being healed, from diseases to limbs growing out where there had been none, hard to deny that kind of evidence. If you have interest in the great healing revivals, as I do, then you will know of hundreds of cases like this. No time to go into this here, that will be another book, but google or read up on Katherine Kuhlman, Kenneth Hagin, Smith Wigglesworth, Reinard Bonke, John G Lake, Alexander Dowie, William Branham etc. As Christians we are supposed to have faith in God, or have God like faith. What is faith, it is the substance of things hoped for, the evidence of things not yet seen. So, if you are a Christian, how do you know you are? You are saved by grace through faith, you have no tangible proof, you can't physically see anything, but you know. The fruit of this will become apparent in your life as you follow your Christian walk. This is no different then to receiving your healing. Ask, believe, and receive, your Heavenly Father will withhold no good thing from those who believe. All good things come down from the Father of lights. Plead the blood of Jesus over your sickness and know with conviction that it is gone. Don't be concerned about how you feel, feelings have little to do with it, keep walking by faith, symptoms may last a while, they sometimes go instantly, but not always. Symptoms are a current fact, but truth trumps fact every time. Jesus said "I am the way, the truth and the life." Put your focus on Jesus where the impossible is easy "Then you will know the truth, and the truth will set you free."

"When you prioritise His presence, He will prioritise you needs, and when His presence is beckoned, His glory will increase. The miraculous is easy, when your focus is on Him, it the atmosphere intended, and the worship from within" (Phil Cawley).

As Christians we are partakers of divine nature. We have the blood of Jesus coursing through us, we have the power of the Holy Spirit living within us. As we daily renew our minds with the word of God we are empowered and taught the mysteries of God by the Holy Ghost. The blood of Jesus is sufficient for us and will supply our every need with the abundance from God's riches in glory.

Another area to be mindful of in claiming our healing is generational or bloodline curses. Generational curses can be passed on for centuries if not checked and dealt with. Thankfully for Christians this is relatively straight forward. Science would tell us that the hereditary nature of diseases and illnesses accounts for a very small percentage. We do know, however, that lifestyle choices, attitudes, behavioural traits, mentality, indecision, bad habits, poor diet, and many other factors are regularly known to be passed down family lines. Behavioural traits like anger, impatience, harboured bitterness, grudges and the like can fester within families. Familiar spirits will attach to these and perpetuate these traits down the family line. Science has clearly proven that things like resentment and bitterness, if not dealt with, will fester and cause not only further resentment, but also manifest in physical infirmity. Addictive behaviours are also commonly passed down the line. Again, if there is alcoholism within a family, familiar spirits will attach to this, if the alcoholic dies, the familiar spirit will look for the next victim to attach itself to. Familiar spirits will attach to sins of all kinds in this way and the vice or addiction or sickness or behavioural trait will be passed down through family lines. Things may appear to be a bad coincidence or misfortune, when in reality they are evil spirits and can be eradicated, permanently.

The family bloodline is cleansed by the pleading of a far superior blood to infuse the situation. The generational curse will be arrested and the person will be free and well and furthermore there will be no further repeat of this down the family line. Pray that the blood of Jesus will cleanse your family line down to this generation and beyond from any bloodline curses in the name of Jesus. (See chapter 12)

Communion (the Lord's Supper)

We were told in scripture to partake of the Lord's supper in remembrance of Jesus. This is a practice which in some churches is weekly, in others it is biweekly or monthly, but it is usually part of most true Christian services. This is a practice that Jesus instigated amongst His disciples. There are different accounts of this remembrance service in the Bible, I will refer to the one in 1 Corinthians 11, "Jesus on the night he was betrayed took bread, broke it, and said this is my body broken for you, do this in remembrance of me. He then took the cup, saying, this cup is the new covenant in my blood, this do as often as you drink it, in remembrance of me. For, whenever you eat the bread and drink the cup you proclaim the Lord's death until He comes". This passage then goes on to stress the importance and the power of these symbolic elements. He states that if you partake of this supper in an unworthy manner, you will be guilty of sinning against the body and blood of the Lord. If you are not discerning of the body and the blood, you are eating and drinking damnation to your soul and bringing judgement upon yourself. The communion service is a very powerful service and many people have been healed and delivered in these meetings when focussing on the shed blood of Jesus. Most people are grateful to receive the communion emblems and are thankful for the forgiveness of sin and this is right. But according to Isaiah 53: 4-5 Jesus' sacrifice was intended to cover all areas of our existence. Jesus suffered physical torture, mental distress, spiritual torment, sorrow, fear, pain and sickness, trauma and distress, He took all of our pains and bore them in the stripes ripped out of His back. "By His stripes we are healed." If we only receive part of His sacrifice, we are doing Jesus a mis-service. We should be receiving and applying the blood in its fullness, accepting everything His blood provided for us, if we don't, as Kenneth Copeland said, we are missing out on all the other benefits that His blood availed for. Paul said that many are weak and fall asleep early because of this lack of discernment.

God does not bring sickness or infirmity to anyone, He has no sickness in Heaven to give; some have a notion that sickness has been given by God to teach them a lesson, but this is untrue. All sickness and disease, infirmities, viruses, depression and mental illnesses come from the devil. Remember his only mission on earth, while he has time, is to steal, kill, and destroy; Jesus came to bring life in abundance. The blood of Jesus, if applied to any of these situations in the correct way and in faith, will bring victory. All evil spirits of sickness and disease and all these strongholds of darkness will be overcome; "we overcome by the blood of the lamb, and the word of our testimony." When we make much of the blood, we get a thicker and more tangible presence of the Holy Spirit. Often at healing conferences, the good ones, the pastor will have many songs about the blood cued up for the evening. In corporate worship, with many voices in one accord singing about the blood, there is immense power and the Holy Spirit seals this with His presence and the atmosphere becomes electric. There is soon an air of excitement and eager anticipation as the Holy Spirit moves among the people, all cards are now on the table, anything and everything is possible.

"When we praise the name of Jesus, when we sing about the blood. We are sealed by the Spirit, and our prayers are understood". (Phil Cawley).

Because of the blood of Jesus, we can come boldly into the presence of God and we are made to be the righteousness of God through Jesus.

7 Freedom in the blood

"For by the blood of Christ we are set free. that is, our sins are forgiven. How great is the grace of God?" (Ephesians 1: 7).

God wants relationship with His people. He loves His children, and He wants us to be able to talk to Him about our needs, hopes and concerns. God did not want His relationship with us to be based on a strict set of rules like it was in the Old Testament where everyone was afraid of Him. God had planned for the new covenant through Jesus Christ as He knew man would fail otherwise. God gave His Son, the most important thing to do, to buy back our freedom that had been lost to the devil in the garden of Eden. "For if the blood of bulls and goats and the ashes of a heifer, sprinkling the unclean, sanctifies for the purifying of flesh, how much more shall the blood of Christ, who through the eternal Spirit offered Himself without spot to God, cleanse your conscience from dead works to serve the living God" (Hebrews 9: 13-14).

Jesus bought our freedom at a great cost, by giving His own life as a ransom for all who believe. Jesus is the way, the truth and the life, and when you know the truth, the truth will set you free (John 8: 32). The Spirit of the Lord is in the blood of Jesus, and where the Spirit of the Lord is, there is freedom (2 Corinthians 3: 7). Jesus brought freedom to mankind in His work on the cross when He defeated all the powers of darkness and took away the keys of sin, death and the grave, we are freed by the shed blood of Jesus. "Whom the Son sets free, is free indeed" (John 8: 36).

The Greek word sozo is a word often used to describe salvation, it is a very loaded and descriptive word and has many translations. This word encompasses all the benefits we gain from the shed blood of Jesus Christ. There is often an assumption that when Jesus died on the cross it was for our salvation and nothing else. This notion could not be further from the truth. Although forgiveness for sins was the central purpose, there was so much more that was purchased for us in that great atonement of affection. Sozo is used over 100 times in the New Testament, and is translated as 'save' 38 times in relation to forgiveness of sins. An example would be "for He shall save [sozo] His people from their sins." (Mathew 1: 21). In essence it describes what has been bought for us through the blood of Jesus. We have been saved from eternal death, we have been healed by the stripes of Jesus and we have been born again to a renewed life through the blood of Jesus. Sozo goes much further beyond the forgiveness of sins according to the Strong's Concordance, and brings in the idea of being physically healed of diseases and delivered from your enemies. So then, when we have salvation, we also have, by definition, access to deliverance, healing and protection. We are not just saved from Hell and the wrath to come. Jesus through the shedding of His blood came to deliver, protect and provide for us in this physical world that we live in now, on earth. If our salvation includes our provision on earth, then by implication it means our prosperity. Jeremiah 29: 11 says "For I know the plans I have for you, declares the Lord, plans to prosper you and not to harm you, plans to give you hope and a future." In the book of Luke 4: 18-19 we read "The Spirit of the Lord is on me, because He has anointed me to proclaim good news to the poor. He has sent me to proclaim freedom for the prisoners."

There are also many occasions when the exact same Greek word meaning saved in the Bible, was translated as healed, they appear to be almost interchangeable. This is referenced in the account of Jairus' daughter in Mark 5: 23, Jairus says to Jesus "I pray Thee, come lay Thy hands on her that she may be healed [sozo]. In this case she died and Jesus raised her, so the word has another layer referring to resurrection also. There are many instances in the Bible where the translation is healed. The healing of the demoniac in Luke: 8 was also this translation, "he had faith to be healed". In this case it applies to healing and deliverance. The same word sozo can be translated as 'made whole' as in the woman with the issue of blood, "thy faith has made thee whole [sozo] (Mathew 9:22). This translation is used over 10 times in the Bible.

Salvation [sozo] then, encompasses forgiveness of sins, deliverance, healing of the body, our mental and physical wellbeing and our financial prosperity. Salvation [sozo] is a massive deal. It doesn't just refer to the forgiveness of sins, as some would believe, this would not be giving this blood bought gift its true and full credit. Forgiveness is the central premise, but there is so much more available for a blood bought believer in Jesus Christ, and why wouldn't there be, this is a gift from the King of Kings who gives abundantly. These gifts from God, all wrapped up in salvation are for believers here and now, they were bought with a great price, there will be no need for them in Heaven, as everything is perfection there.

The blood of Jesus then has given us freedom in all areas of our lives. We are free from the sting of death, free from sickness and disease, free from harm, free from demonic attack, free from lack and poverty, free to worship and serve a mighty God. "Since the children have flesh and blood, He too shared their humanity, so that by His death He might break the power of him who holds the power of death, the devil, and free those who all their lives were held in slavery by their fear of death." (Hebrews 2: 14-15) Jesus came to bind up the broken hearted, to proclaim liberty to the captives and freedom to the prisoners (Isaiah 61: 1).

"To Him who loves us and has freed us from our sins by His blood" (Revelation 1: 5).

8   Hedge of protection

"Have you not put a hedge around Him and his household, and everything he has? You have blessed the work of his hands, so that his flocks and herds spread throughout the land" (Job :1: 10).

The blood builds a hedge of protection around us, it is our security, our protection against the forces of evil. "He that digs a pit shall fall into it, and he who breaks the hedge, the serpent will bite him" (Ecclesiastes 10: 8). We must plead the blood over our families and homes and pray the hedge of protection around them. Job chapter 1 explains the areas of protection the blood gives us. The hedge of protection in the blood, covers you, your family, your home, your possessions, your endeavours and your influence, says Benny Hinn. As a child of God, you have a right to the protection of the blood of Jesus. As mentioned earlier in this book, the sacrificial lamb in the account of the Passover was a symbol of Jesus, and the sacrifice He would later make for mankind. It is a theme echoed within the practice of communion, or 'the Lord's supper' in church services. The lamb was sacrificed, and its blood was painted onto the doorposts of the houses of the Israelites. The blood was the protective signal to the angel of death that came to kill all the firstborn sons of the Egyptians. He saw the blood and spared them, he passed over their homes and they were safe. The blood of the lamb was purely symbolic, it had no power in its self, the power was embedded in what the blood represented. The angel of death didn't see the lambs blood smeared on the doorposts, he saw the blood of The Lamb, slain from the foundation of the world. A spirit of death has to bow and admit defeat before the blood of Jesus, it cannot enter the home of anyone who has this covering. No powers or principalities, or any forces of the kingdom of darkness can come upon you, they must pass by, they have no authority, they must bow to the far superior power of Jesus. The blood of the lamb is inexhaustible and unlimited, and when we apply the blood in faith over our lives, we access the power to defeat all curses or powers that wish to have influence. We double up on this power by pleading the blood in the name of Jesus as the blood is behind the name and we are fully protected.

The devil knows only too well the power in the blood and the name of Jesus. Kenneth Copeland told of an account of Billye Brim's son Chip. He had been preaching one evening and a demon possessed witch doctor was present at the meeting. The witch doctor kept trying to attack a group of Pastors who had spent hours trying to calm her down. She spotted Chip and launched to attack him, he shouted at her saying

"I plead the blood!". She instantly cowered away, covering her ears and saying "not the blood". The ministers then quickly calmed her down, declaring the blood of Jesus and she was delivered within 15 minutes. Demons and devils hate the blood of Jesus and the name of Jesus, it is so powerful. The blood will keep the devil out of the affairs of your life but it must be pleaded in faith.

I remember reading Billye Brim's book The Blood and the Glory, many years ago, it has had a profound effect on me until this day. In this book Billye explains about the circular nature of the bloodline of God. God shed the first blood in the garden of Eden to make a covering for Adam and Eve. The precious blood was manifest on earth when Jesus came, and then He poured out for mankind on the cross at Calvery. The circle turned upwards again when Jesus conquered death and carried His own precious blood back to Heaven when He ascended and there it remains ever speaking mercy for mankind.

Billye tells of an incident involving a minister and his wife in Canada. They had been conducting meetings in a large church there and had left the children at home in the US with their grandparents. These meetings were very powerful and many people were being saved and delivered from the powers of darkness. The devil became infuriated with this minister and began to torment him with thoughts that he was going to kill his children while he was away preaching. The minister exclaimed 'devil you're a liar, you cannot kill my children'. The devil impressed in the thoughts of the minister that he had put rabid foxes in the wood adjourning his property. Immediately the minister remembered that friends had seen foxes roaming on his land before he left his home in Tennessee. The minister gathered together three other believers and together they agreed in prayer, by faith, and they drew a bloodline of protection around the minister's property. A week later the minister received a letter from his brother saying; he had been out walking around the edge of the property and he found five dead foxes. These foxes were examined and were found to be carrying rabies, they had died when they tried to cross the bloodline.

In biblical times, perimeter fencing was often not made of stone or wood, but rather of hedges. The hedges were constructed of low, intertwined thorn bushes placed close together and growing around the homestead. These hedges were strong and the thorns were sharp to the touch, and would keep livestock from leaving and wild animals from entering. This is the kind of hedge that is referred to in Job 10, and would have been commonplace in those days. A hedge of protection, impenetrable to any unwanted guests. The hedge is a boundary designed to serve as a covering or shield, to protect us from exposure to danger, damage, injury, harm or any destruction to our household. No devils or demons can pass through a hedge of protection put in place by God. Psalm 91 tell us that "Whoever dwells in the shelter of the Most- High, will rest in the shadow of the Almighty."

The Bible tells us that God has given us promises of protection, and these are all owed to the shedding of the blood of Jesus. John 10: 28-30 says that no one can snatch you out of the Fathers hand. When we plead the blood of Jesus, we gain access to all of God's promises, so we can affirm; "The angel of the Lord encamps around those who fear Him, and He delivers them" (Psalm 34: 7). Again, in Psalm 5: 11 we read "Let all who take refuge in you be glad; let them ever sing for joy. Spread Your protection over them, that those who love Your name may rejoice in You." Pray to God and plead the blood over the protection of your family, livelihood and your home, there is so much power in the blood. God has promised so often to protect you from things meant for your harm. He will watch over your family, provide shelter and safety in times of trouble, and put His hedge of protection around you when the enemy attacks. There will be times of sorrow in life, but this does not negate the promises of God, this is purely because we live in a fallen world.

God will often be instrumental in protecting us from ourselves. Our will power will sometimes fail us, our desire to do good, and achieve what we know we should, sometimes falters; just like Paul explains in Romans 7, the good that I want to do, I don't do. God can hedge us out of the things which are not good for us to pursue, making it difficult to get along, and giving us a wake- up call. Plead the blood over your protection and know that "if you say the Lord is my refuge, and you make the Most-High your dwelling, no harm will overtake you, no disaster will come near your tent" (Psalm 91: 9-10). God's hedge of protection is a safe place for us, but it does not mean we should allow ourselves to take it for granted and behave in ways that would compromise it. If our lifestyle becomes weakened by following the wrong paths, we can compromise our safety, and the devil again gains legal right to come into the camp. We can never be separated ultimately from the love of God but we can compromise our safety here on earth. In the book of Zachariah 2: 5 God is speaking to Israel but as Christians we are also the children of God, so this verse is just as applicable to us. The verse says "And I myself will be a wall of fire around it, declares the Lord, and I will be its glory within".

"The atonement of affection, put the power into our faith, and through the blood, a hedge of protection, a wall of fire is going to keep us safe" (P. Cawley).

Pleading with the blood and the name of Jesus is highly effective in our spiritual warfare. Devils and demons cower in terror at the sound of the blood and the name of Jesus, praying in tongues and calling on the fire of the Holy Spirit, all will add to the strength of the hedge of protection around your family and household. John Ramirez, is a powerful evangelist and ex-devil worshipper and has many times talked about the power of the blood. John has stated that when a Christian knows who they are under the blood of Jesus, no amount of devilry and witchcraft can penetrate. He said it was easy to overcome weak Christians, but when he came up against the power of the blood his powers were ineffective and he could not break through those powerful prayers of the saints. John said that on one occasion he was trying to use witchcraft on a woman and for some reason it would not work, he was frustrated with this and took it to the devil. The devil said to him 'her God will not allow any harm to come to her'.

If you know how to defend yourself spiritually by using the blood of Jesus, you can live a life of victory under the complete protection of God. We are in constant spiritual warfare in a world that is living with the consequences of the Adamic curse and the fall of mankind. We are up against the devil and his hoards who are on assignment to steal, kill and destroy, and they will if we are not practicing with the tools of our protection. It is no good having a state-of-the-art security system but not flipping the switch, there needs to be a power source. Appropriate the blood of Jesus over your life and walk in the full protection and power that its covering provides.

9 Feasting on the blood

"Then Jesus declared, I am the bread of life. Whoever comes to me will never go hungry, and whoever believes in me will never thirst."

Without food and drink as human beings we very quickly die. We can survive without food for maybe a couple of months while wasting away, but only 3 days without water. We need to eat and drink to gain our physical nourishment, and we need to do this regularly to sustain us. This seems obvious, that we need physical nourishment, but we need spiritual nourishment even more so. "Man shall not live by bread alone, but by every word that proceeds from the mouth of God" (Mathew 4: 4).

In John chapter 6 there is a very important message that Jesus is trying to get over to His disciples and the Jewish people and leaders. The chapter begins with the 'Feeding of the five thousand', where Jesus feeds the multitude with two small fish and five loaves of bread. That evening Jesus performs more miracles, He is seen by His disciples walking to them on the water, and then when he gets in the boat, they are all instantly transported to the other side of the lake. The following day some of the same people go looking for Jesus and find Him on the other side of the lake. Jesus now expands on His message, saying, you look for me, not because of the signs you saw, but because you ate and had your fill. He warns them "do not work for food that spoils, but for food that endures to eternal life, which the Son of Man will give you, for on Him, God the Father has placed His approval."

Jesus was telling the people that He is our source of food and life, and then He gave one of the most controversial messages in the Bible. "Jesus said to them, most assuredly I say to you, unless you eat the flesh of the Son of Man and drink His blood, you have no life in you. Whoever eats my flesh and drinks my blood has eternal life, and I will raise him up at the last day. For my flesh is food indeed, and my blood is drink indeed. He who eats My flesh and drinks My blood abides in Me and I in Him As the living Father sent Me, and I live because of the Father, so he who feeds on me will live because of me" (John 6: 53-57).

Many of His followers were offended by these statements and began to leave. This is the offense of the cross, the message of the blood of Jesus being shed is always one that divides the spiritually minded from the carnal minded people. Jesus said, "I am the living bread that came down from Heaven, whoever eats this bread will live forever. This bread is my flesh, which I will give for the life of the world" (John 6: 51).

The disciples found this message hard and wondered who could accept it. Jesus explained to His disciples that it is the Spirit that brings life, the flesh amounts to nothing, the words I speak to you, He said are spirit and life. Jesus is talking about spiritual discernment, eating His flesh and drinking His blood spiritually, to gain spiritual, and eternal nourishment. This is referring to taking Jesus and His soul cleansing blood into our innermost being, spirit and soul. Then Jesus, seeing that many followers had turned and left, said to the twelve disciples, "do you want to leave too?", Peter answered Him saying "Lord to whom shall we go, You have the words of eternal life. We have come to believe that You are the Holy One of God" (John 6: 68).

We feed on God then by reading, studying and digesting His word, by believing in Him and applying our faith. His blood and flesh were given as a sacrifice for us at the cross, when we are weak, we need to return to this and reflect. We will find renewed strength when we partake of the body and the blood of Jesus. We receive power when we partake of the sacrifice Jesus made for us, it is more than enough to cover every area of our lives, to give us life and health and deliver us from all evil.

Eating and drinking the body and blood of Jesus is drawing close to Jesus and fervently believing that the abuse of His body and the shedding of Hs blood fully paid for our sins. Jesus put the Lord Supper, or communion, in place so that we always remember what is at the very centre or core of our belief. Without the sacrificial bloodshed of the spotless Lamb of God, Jesus Christ, we would be left in our sin and there would be no Christianity. All these discourses that Jesus has with His followers are embedding the principles of the Lamb slain from the foundations of the world. It was always the master plan of God, Jesus talked about His own death often with His disciples and uses many preparatory doctrines and truths in the time preceding His death. Don't be like the carnal minded crowds who came to Jesus for sign, wonders and physical food. Be like Peter, discerning that Jesus holds the words of eternal life and that all other paths in life will be temporary and short lived at best.

10   Judged by the blood

"How much more severely do you think someone deserves to be punished who has trampled the Son of God underfoot; who has treated as an unholy thing the blood of the covenant that sanctified them, and who has insulted the Spirit of grace. For we know Him who said, 'it is mine to avenge, I will repay'. The Lord will judge His people" (Hebrews 10: 29-30).

Before moving into this chapter, let's just clear up a few myths and level out some misguided theories and doctrines. Let's lay to rest some ugly rumours that there are many ways to God. All paths and religions do not lead to God, no matter what others may tell you. You will not make it by just being a good person, though being a good person is an admirable virtue. Reincarnation and Karma, though interesting theories, will not get you there. The Islamic religion of good works is a bit closer to the truth, but Jesus is not a Muslim prophet. Spiritualism is abhorrent to God. New Age notions of spiritual and holistic idealism, transcendental Karma, paganism, or occult practices, no matter how devout the practitioner, will not end well.

Jesus said "I am the way, the truth and the life, no one comes to the Father except through me" (John 14: 6).

"Jesus, the Son of God, the word, took on flesh and came to live among us. We have seen His glory, the glory of the one and only Son, who came from the Father, full of grace and truth." (John 1: 14). He came into the world to save sinners as the world is a fallen world. "If you confess with your mouth Jesus is Lord, and believe in your heart that God raised Him from the dead, you will be saved" (Romans 10: 9). "For the blood of Jesus Christ, God's son cleanses us from all sin" (1 John 1: 7).

The judgement of God is also in the blood of Jesus. Because of what Jesus accomplished on the cross by shedding His blood, believers are redeemed, the price has been paid. So, when God looks down on us, He doesn't see our sinful nature, all he sees is the blood covering of Jesus. Everyone who refuses to accept the blood sacrifice of Jesus will be judged according to their sins and will perish. Despite the great sacrifice made by God to send His son to die a hideous death on our behalf, He made salvation so easy for us. The deciding factor on whether your eternal future is in Heaven or Hell is not about what you did or didn't do with your life on earth. It doesn't matter how much of a villain you were, how much of a Hell raiser or criminal you were. It doesn't matter, in this sense, if you committed heinous crimes against your fellow man. The Apostle Paul, who is responsible for a significant part of the New Testament, started out persecuting and killing Christians. Acts chapter 9 tells us of his miraculous conversion when Jesus spoke to him on the Damascus Road. Paul spent the rest of his life preaching Jesus Christ, or writing from his jail cell. It equally is of little consequence if you lived on earth like a saint, doing good to all you meet, karma is just a word.

The big question, the only question, deciding your eternal future of Heaven or Hell, is what did you make of Jesus Christ. If you lived an evil life, but truly repented, and confessed Jesus as Lord, you will be saved, just as the model citizen will be saved on the confession of their sins also. "We have all sinned and fallen short of the glory of God" (Romans 3: 23). This may seem a little unfair, but often those who have been forgiven much, love much and show greater thankfulness and forgiveness to others. "Let him who is without sin cast the first stone" (John 8: 7).

11 Why plead the blood

When you plead the blood of Jesus against the kingdom of darkness, you are enforcing the judgement of God on those demonic forces. You are declaring that the blood of Jesus has spoiled them, made a show of them openly and defeated them. Pleading the blood is a legal process, just like a Lawyer pleading a case in court. When the 'accuser of the brethren' or the devil says we are guilty, we plead before God with the blood and are declared not guilty.

When we plead the blood, we also claim authority over Satan and keep him out of all our affairs. The devil has no rights when we plead the blood because of Calvery, and we have every right to walk in His provision. We know from Hebrews 12: 24 that Jesus is our mediator in the new covenant and that the sprinkled blood speaks a better word than the blood of Abel. In the book of Genesis, Abel had been murdered by his brother and his blood was crying to God for revenge. The blood of Jesus, conversely, brings us forgiveness. 1 Peter 1: 2 shows that we were chosen by God the Father through the sanctifying work of the Spirit, to be obedient to Jesus Christ and sprinkled with His blood. We are repeatedly told that we have a right to being covered by the blood.

When you plead the blood then, be definite about what you are pleading it over and know that it will have profound effect. If you have a specific health issue, then name it and rebuke the spirit of infirmity or oppression that is behind it in Jesus name. We always ask in the name of Jesus so that our joy may be made complete. The blood of Jesus speaks, and the name of Jesus forces the enemy to bow, giving you the victory. This two- pronged attack on the devil cannot fail; the demons and devils tremble at the sound, you can curse demon entities by the blood and the name.

Applying the blood of Jesus is the most potent and powerful weapon in the Christian armoury. It is essential if we value our protection to use this weapon daily. Living in these uncertain days of viral pandemic and global unrest it is more important than ever to ensure you have divine protection. Plead the blood over your homes and families, your property and possessions, your finances, business and ministry. When we acknowledge and appropriate all the provisions of the cross, we will be victorious. Redemption and healing, protection and forgiveness, deliverance, provision and power are all ours through the blood.

Pleading the blood of Jesus is an offensive prayer, we are not defending our health, possessions, families etc, we are stating our claim to divine protection. We are saying to the devil and his minions that we are covered by the blood in all areas of our lives, you will not come near me. We should not be living defeated lives as Christians; the devil will come at you at times in your life but instead of battening down the hatches we should be ready to attack and remind him of who we are because of the blood. "Be alert and of sober mind. Your enemy the devil prowls around like a roaring lion looking for someone to devour" (1 Peter 5: 8). As Christians, however, we have been given "the authority to trample on serpents and scorpions, and over all the power of the enemy, and nothing shall by any means harm us" (Luke 10: 19). As Spirit-filled believers we have supernatural power to come against anything trying to harm us. Anything intent on bringing us harm is demonic, he comes only to steal, kill and destroy. So, this would include any harm to our health, families, homes, possessions, ministries, businesses, and anything we hold dear. We have blood bought authority to trample on such forces, and we do this by pleading the blood of Jesus and using His name. We plead the blood daily in all key areas of our lives before the event, as well as during, it's like setting up state of the art security systems in our homes or cars. The demonic forces cannot come near, they will see the blood and flee. They will move on to an easier target as they will see you have been given a heads up on their strategy, and that you are well versed in applying a far superior power.

I have a great deal of respect for John Ramirez, Author and Evangelist. He was one of the highest-ranking devil worshippers in New York and the surrounding areas, John really knows his stuff. Having been a very effective ambassador for the devil for over 20 years he knows the demonic strategies very well. John explained that he used to astral project over many different neighbourhoods and curse the areas, churches and communities. John said this was fairly easy for him and he was successful in this. One night however he was astral projecting over a certain neighbourhood and he came across a group of Spirit filled Christians who knew the power of the blood, John said his satanic powers were useless against them and he left defeated. John could carry out the devil's work in strength and confidence, but if he came into contact with Christians who knew the power of the blood and the name of Jesus, he was stripped of his power. John is now an extremely effective General in the service of God. He preaches and teaches world-wide and has written many awesome books on living in victory and defeating his old father the devil. I can not do John justice in a short page of a book. I would strongly suggest you search him out, check out his books and watch his services and discussions on You tube.

12 Applying & pleading the blood

If you are not a Christian, then firstly well done for getting through this far. This subject matter is often avoided even in Christian circles, so, thanks for taking the time and I hope you found it interesting, even if you have not experienced the power yet.

If you want to become a Christian, based on what you have read, then there is a very easy process I would like you to follow. Again, don't worry about how you feel afterwards, often people don't feel a thing, this is faith not feelings.

Repeat this affirmation and speak it from your heart. Lord Jesus, I give you my heart, and all that is within me, I ask for You to come into my life as my Lord and Saviour. Deliver me from the power of sin and help me to live for You. In Jesus name. All done, now the journey begins.

A short prayer each morning:

Father I plead the blood of Jesus over my life and the lives of my immediate and wider family in Jesus name. Father I plead the blood over my home, my car and all my material possessions. I plead the blood over my health and that of my family, my finances, my business, my ministry, and my church. Father I draw a bloodline around my home, and those of my family, with the blood of Jesus, and I declare that no evil or demonic spirits can penetrate this line, it is a wall of fire, and gives total protection. Father I plead the blood of Jesus over my health from the top of my head to the souls of my feet, no illness, virus or disease can come upon me in Jesus name. Father I plead the blood of Jesus over this day, and over all my endeavours, I am protected in all my ways and no harm can befall me in Jesus name. Father I plead the blood over my mind will and emotions, I have a spirit of power, love and a sound mind. I am blessed with wisdom, knowledge, discernment and understanding, creativity and divine inspiration in Jesus name. Thankyou Father for answered prayer. I am so grateful that through the blood of Jesus I am free, clean and healed, I am blessed, delivered, protected and prospered, in Jesus name. Amen

More detailed application:

I plead the blood of Jesus over my physical body, over my spirit and over my mind, will and emotions. I plead the blood over any demonic forces who may try to come against me, any evil forces of any kind; any illnesses, viruses, diseases or accidents that may cross my path. I have full faith and conviction that the blood of Jesus will cover me and keep me from all harm. I will overcome all evil by the blood of the Lamb and the word of my testimony. The blood has the power to protect me against any weapon formed against me, and nothing designed for my harm will prosper. The blood of Jesus avails for me with power to restore what the locust has eaten; it enables me to forgive and to be forgiven and provides for all of my needs.

I plead the blood over my family and loved ones, my home, car and all my material possessions. I plead the blood over my relationships, my finances, my business, my income and investments, my ministry, my country, my community and my church.

I plead the blood of Jesus to break the power of any assignments the kingdom of darkness may have formed against me or any member of my family in Jesus name. I cancel every evil plan that has been established in opposition to God's plan for my life. I come against all generational curses in my bloodline, and I dissolve, and eradicate them through the power of Jesus blood. The blood of Jesus speaks a better word and apply it to my bloodline in Jesus name. I plead the blood over any familiar spirits that would attach themselves to me to bring any curses, ill health or destructive behaviour to my life. I break the bloodline curse by the redemptive healing power of the blood of Jesus in Jesus mighty name. Any and all demonic powers that are standing watch over my family to perpetuate the curse, I destroy by the power of the blood of Jesus, I release the fire of the Holy Ghost in Jesus name. Father restore unto me all the years that the locust has eaten sevenfold as Your word has said. Restore Your divine favour to my life and give me the joy of the Lord, in Jesus name.

Father I come against all spirits of infirmity with the blood of Jesus. I fully receive all the benefits of the redemptive power of the blood of Jesus and his death on the cross. You bore all of my sins and healed me by Your stripes, righteousness shall arise with healing in His wings. Father I curse the root of every infirmity in my body and I apply the blood that speaks healing over me in the name of Jesus. Father I ask for and receive the release of supernatural strength into my body right now by the power of the blood of Jesus. Father if any symptoms still exist, I disregard them in Jesus name, temporary fact is far inferior to the power of Your wonderful truth, and Your word says I am healed by the stripes of Jesus. My mind is made up, I am walking by faith, I am covered by the blood and waiting for my physical body to catch up with spiritual reality.

I declare that my body is a temple of the Holy Spirit, I am clean, healed, forgiven, sanctified, refined, perfected and protected by the blood of Jesus. God goes before me and lives within me and His Angels are encamped all around me.

I declare excellence of soul and divine and supernatural health, because the blood of Jesus gives me life and divine protection. I plead the blood of Jesus against all the powers and schemes of the enemy. I bind all the powers of darkness, every spell, curse, or oath taken against me or negative words spoken against me in Jesus name. I break the yoke of the evil one and his many entities. I break the power of anxiety, depression and confusion, sadness, sorrow and bitterness. I break the power of unforgiveness, resent and offense through the blood of Jesus. I break any powers or rebellious spirits that come against my family, relationships, marriage, work or ministry in Jesus name.

I plead the blood of Jesus over any entities that would entice me into unfruitful relationships or into bad or destructive habits. I draw a blood line in Jesus blood around my home and that of my family; a hedge of protection, a wall of fire that cannot be penetrated.

I put all evil forces on notice of eviction, no evil spirits of witchcraft, occult, spiritualism or any other repulsive or rebellious entities can cross the blood line, I send you back to the dry and arid places you came from. There is all power in the blood of the Lamb. Thank You Father for answered prayer. I am so grateful that through the blood of Jesus I am free, clean and healed, I am blessed, delivered, protected and prospered, in Jesus name. Amen

These are all encompassing prayers and may be too much for your life situation, they are just to give you ideas and a place to start. Feel free to use these as they are or cut and adapt them to better suit your individual circumstances then enjoy living in freedom and victory.

Another very effective way of pleading the blood is to place your hands on the thing you are pleading for, like your possessions. Put your hands on the car, or get inside the car and plead the blood over it, declaring that it works efficiently and will not come into harm's way on the road. You can also do this over your property, by walking through it, and also around its perimeter and pleading the blood over its protection. We have power over all the power of the enemy and nothing shall be able to harm us.

Plead the blood over your health:

Father Your word says that you desire above all things that I should prosper and be in health, and that by the stripes of Jesus I am healed. So, Father I plead the blood of Jesus over my body, and ask that its healing power would course through my veins bringing life to every cell. Father I declare that every fibre of my being, from the top of my head, to the souls of my feet be energised, revitalised and purified in Jesus name. Father I declare that my body is in perfect vibration with Heaven. I am created in the image of God, and no illness or infirmity can come upon me because the blood avails for me, I declare divine health in Jesus name. Father I declare that any evil entities with assignment on my physical or mental health, are evicted now in Jesus name. I am covered by the blood of Jesus and I have a hedge of protection around me and my family that no demon or devil can cross. Father I know that spiritual warfare begins in the mind, this is where the devil likes to attack; if he can get to my thoughts and my words, he can steer the whole ship. So, Father, I plead the blood over my thought life, I take every thought captive in Jesus name. Thoughts become things, as a man thinks in his heart, so is he. Father I plead the blood over my internal dialogue and focus on things of good report, so that no bitterness, unforgiveness or offense can fester within me and weaken me. I have a spirit of power, love and a sound mind in Jesus name. Father I plead the blood of Jesus over my entire cellular makeup and immune system. No foreign viruses can enter, no mutation of cells will occur and my immunity is impenetrable in Jesus name. Father I thank You that I will prosper and be in divine health, even as my soul prospers, in Jesus name, Amen.

Plead the blood for provision:

Father, You are Jehovah Jireh, my provider and I shall lack nothing. Jesus died so that I can have full access to You and Your heavenly provision. Because of Jesus blood I am legally entitled to all Your wonderful promises. Father I plead the blood of Jesus over my work, my business and all my financial affairs; I am assured that because of the blood You will supply all of my needs according to Your riches in glory and I am expectant that they will manifest in my life in Jesus name. Let Your kingdom come, and Your will be done in my life, just as it is in Heaven. Thank You Father for providing for all of my needs, in Jesus name Amen.

Conclusion

We now understand that blood is life, the life of every living being is encompassed within the blood. If someone has disease of some kind in their blood it will quickly affect the whole body and the person will become sick. Blood is an intricate transport and communication system, keeping all parts informed, healthy, nourished and protected.

Jesus blood, unlike any other, is all powerful and provides a divine covering for our sin. This has been demonstrated throughout the Bible and I have given evidence of this throughout the book. The shedding of blood in the Old Testament was pleasing to God as an atonement for the sins of men, as it was symbolic of the sacrifice Jesus was destined to make, as a one-time atonement. Man's sin continued throughout Bible history and the sacrifice of animals was no longer enough. The next part of God's master plan was soon to be required. Jesus was born, and came to earth for a very short time. For 33 years, God in the flesh, walked the earth in preparation for a 3-year period of ministry, and to ultimately give His life for the love of mankind to reconcile all of them to God.

Science tells us that living matter cannot be destroyed, it can only be transformed into other forms of existence. When we eat our food, it is full of live bacteria, we take from it what our body needs to thrive and the rest will ultimately end up back in the ground. The ground then produces other living organisms and so the life cycle continues. The blood of Jesus shed on the cross continues to live in healing power, and it is available to all who choose to tap into the everlasting, eternal supply. Jesus blood covers the whole of creation, bringing life to the world, to the universe. It has always been there, the Lamb slain from the foundation of the world, to avail for everyone who seeks it. It is available to everyone, believers and unbelievers alike have been healed by the blood of Jesus, healing usually would result in salvation due to the grace of God.

Pleading the blood of Jesus is one of the most effective ways to pray. When you are praying about something, and then you plead the blood over that thing, a divine transaction takes place. You are now not only bringing to God something very important to you, you are bringing it covered in the blood of Jesus. How could the Father not hear and answer your prayers when they are covered in the precious blood of His Son, the blood that speaks a much better word. When God sees the blood that was shed for the forgiveness, the healing, the deliverance, the prosperity and provision of man, He will honour your request. Jesus blood bought us full access to God. "Therefore, brothers and sisters, since we have the confidence to enter the most Holy place by the blood of Jesus, by a new and living way, opened to us through the curtain that is His body, and since we have a great price over the house of God. Let us draw near to God with a sincere heart, and with the full assurance that faith brings, having our hearts sprinkled to cleanse us from a guilty conscience and having our bodies washed with pure water. Let us hold unswervingly to the hope we profess, for He who promised is faithful" (Hebrews 10: 19-23).

Jesus blood is all powerful, it represents the supreme offering to God to reconcile the sins of men. "For God presented Jesus as the sacrifice for sin. People are made right with God when they believe that Jesus sacrificed His life, shedding His blood" (Romans 3: 25). It has the power to give us freedom, "All glory to Him who loves us and has freed us from our sins by shedding Hs blood for us" (Revelation 1: 5). His blood justifies us, "Since therefore, we have now been justified by His blood, how much more shall we be saved by Him from the wrath of God" (Romans 5: 9). We can be cleansed by the blood, "Just think how much more the blood of Christ will purify our conscience from sinful deeds, so that we can worship the living God" (Hebrews 9: 14). We can be sanctified by the blood "Jesus also suffered outside the gate in order to sanctify the people through His own blood" (Hebrews 13:12). We are brought closer to God and can enter boldly into Heaven's most Holy place because of the blood. We are also given peace, "He made peace with everything in Heaven and on earth by means of Christs blood on the cross" (Colossians 19: 20). We are given full protection through the blood, "And they overcame him (the devil) by the blood of the Lamb and by the word of their testimony" (Revelation 12: 11).

Christians are powerless unless they are fully aware of who they are through the blood. Once they have this truth deep within them, all that the blood bought for them, then no weapon formed against them will prosper. Blood is just a word until it is used, ammunition is only powerful when it's locked and loaded, shells are no good left in the box.

Pleading or applying the blood of Jesus in your prayer time is offensive praying, taking it to the devil, staking your claim on what was bought for you on the cross. Through the blood, you have legal rights as a Christian. Securing your eternal future is not the only thing bought for you. Your protection, healing, deliverance, provision, freedom, forgiveness and prosperity are all purchased as well.

"For the weapons of our warfare are not carnal, but mighty through God to the pulling down of strongholds" (2 Corinthians 10: 4).

The Blood of The Lamb

"There is power in the blood of the lamb. Scarlet flow like a stream, every heart to redeem, there is power in the blood of the lamb.

There is life in the blood of the lamb. If you're broken, don't you know, there is life in the flow, there is life in the blood of the lamb.

You know your God paid the price for you. He sent His Son to die the worse, and through the pain and undue torture, His blood was spilled to lift the curse.

There is healing in the blood of the lamb. And there's no devil in Hell, strong enough to dispel, that there's healing in the blood of the lamb.

There is peace in the blood of the lamb, you'll be calm through the flood, when you plead with the blood, there is peace in the blood of the lamb".
(Phil Cawley)

Other books by this author

Becoming the Real You:

Did you ever want to rewrite your story, go back to the original book, where nothing is impossible, and with childlike faith, live life like you cannot fail. Your history doesn't have to be your future, break the generational chains and be a trailblazer, cut out a new path for yourself and those who follow. Instead of being a victim of circumstance, you can change your mind-set by thinking in a different way and can create your own reality, be prosperous, happy, healthy and content. Limitations of your past do not have to play a part in shaping your future. Break free from the environmental shackles and perceived obstacles of your external world. Take time every morning to get in touch with your real self and your source, this is the best use of your time to begin each day, to feel connected and at peace with God and with your surroundings. Become the creative and inspired person you are meant to be, truly grateful for all your blessings, and excited for the day that you have planned to unfold. Your thoughts become your words, which in turn influence your actions and lifestyle. Thoughts do become things, and how you harness them will determine your level of success, your health, happiness, spiritual connectedness, your temperament and ultimately your longevity. It is crucial to get this right if you wish to achieve true freedom, fulfil your destiny and become the best versions of yourself. This is your life, don't be a passenger. This book presents selected nuggets of wisdom for personal and spiritual growth. Ideas and strategies to incorporate into your everyday lifestyle to get the most from each day by changing your approach from initial thought to creating your desired reality. An examination of inspirational thought from The Bible, from leaders in Neurological science and Quantum Physics, from selected Authors and Academics and motivational speakers. This book is intended to condense much research and study and scientific evidence supporting the importance of correct thinking, how we use our words, the interplay of the conscious and sub-conscious mind and auto-suggestion. The book assesses the benefits of understanding these key elements and using them correctly to create your desired life, to fulfil your dreams and destiny and become the best you can be. This book encompasses the use of faith and positive thinking to rid yourself of bad habits and move towards a more prosperous life, improving health, wealth, opportunity, happiness, spiritual and personal creativity and achievement. There is much instruction in the use of positive affirmation and visualisation and how these will embed enlightened thought and carefully chosen words. Imagination plays a vital role, as it fuels your dreams, and when combined with an attitude of gratitude from a humble and forgiving heart it puts you in the perfect vibrational frequency to achieve your goals, to attract your aspirational equivalent. This book also has much to say about faith and the avoidance of fear, anxiety and victim mentality, there are many direct quotes from the Bible and many other inspirational thinkers. To become the real you, and be the best version of yourself, there has to be serious consideration given to health and fitness. This book takes a thorough look at the importance of health and wellbeing, diet, supplementation, intermittent fasting and exercise. The book culminates in an example of a typical mighty morning. This chapter includes a walk-through of a typical morning, with examples, of how to get energised mentally, spiritually, physically, and emotionally before most people even start their day.

Be Inspired: Volume 1

Wise words to encourage, move and motivate, to breathe life, spark ideas and impassion your day.

Wise and wonderful words from positive thinkers is a tonic to the heart and soul and gears us up, mentally and physically, for what is ahead. When we reframe our thinking, we can look at our situations differently, and when we change the way we look at things, the things we look at change. A refreshing injection of positive thought can revitalise our thought processes and make us resonate with the joys of life and with new focus on getting the best for our lives and that of others. "Make positive thinking your new habit and enjoy the feeling of being back in control, feeling empowered, encouraged inspired and with renewed faith that you can achieve all you can imagine." Phil Cawley

This inspirational collection of quotes, some famous, some not so well known, will be a great companion for many situations. Your morning devotions, coffee breaks at work, a little book to pack in your holiday bag, your daily commute to and from work or to have on hand for your toilet breaks. "A word of encouragement given at the right time, can, to the recipient, be a veritable gold mine". Phil Cawley

Be Inspired – Volume 2

"Reframe your internal dialogue and unlock your gifting. These inspired quotes are taken from various original writings, musings and songs of mine over many years and would be a great companion for many situations. Your morning devotions, coffee breaks at work, a little book to pack in your holiday bag or for your daily commute to and from work. "A word of encouragement given at the right time, can, to the recipient, be a veritable gold mine".

"Make positive thinking your new habit and enjoy the feeling of being back in control, feeling empowered, encouraged. Inspired and with renewed faith that you can achieve all you can imagine".

Prayers, Affirmations, Musings & Songs Volume 1 & 2

"No defeat and no limitations, I hold the wisdom of ages inside. Everything works for good, I am free through the blood, and I'm washed in that soul cleansing tide."

Reciting Christian truths, songs and affirmations or pondering on them quietly, has a remarkable and uplifting effect bringing our thought life into a higher vibrational frequency and into closer connection with God.

Christian quotes will inspire creativity and encourage us to take action, they energise us, breathing insight and wisdom into our daily lives. They bring happiness, hope and positivity and elevate mood when we need a lift. This selection of Christian inspirational quotes gives original, bite sized verses which are easy to read and retain, they are concise expressions which engender confidence and faith, and the belief that you can succeed in running your race and fulfilling your destiny. Reading insightful words from someone who has climbed the mountain that you are at the foot of, can be invaluable to spur you on to your own success.

Printed in Great Britain
by Amazon